SUPER RABBIT ALL-STARS!

READ MORE
PRESS START!
BOOKS!

MORE BOOKS COMING SOON!

PRESS START!

SUPER RABBIT ALL-STARS!

THOMAS FLINTHAM

BRANCHES

SCHOLASTIC INC.

FOR LEICESTER JOE

All rights reserved. Published by Scholastic Inc. *Publishers since 1920.* SCHOLASTIC, BRANCHES, and associated logos are trademarks and/or registered trademarks of Scholastic Inc.

The publisher does not have any control over and does not assume any responsibility for author or third-party websites or their content.

This book is a work of fiction. Names, characters, places, and incidents are either the product of the author's imagination or are used fictitiously, and any resemblance to actual persons, living or dead, business establishments, events, or locales is entirely coincidental.

Library of Congress Cataloging-in-Publication Data

Flintham, Thomas, author, illustrator. | Flintham, Thomas. Press start! ; 8.
Title: Super Rabbit All-Stars! / by Thomas Flintham.
Description: First edition. | New York, NY : Branches/Scholastic Inc., 2020.
| Series: Press start! ; 8 | Summary: It is time for the All-Star games,
and Super Rabbit Boy wants to be crowned the Ultimate All-Star Champion,
but with so many contestants, including the evil King Viking, he will need
help from Sunny and his video game console to claim his prize.
Identifiers: LCCN 2019007651 | ISBN 9781338239843 (pbk. : alk. paper) | ISBN
9781338239850 (hardcover : alk. paper)
Subjects: LCSH: Superheroes—Juvenile fiction. | Supervillains—Juvenile
fiction. | Animals—Juvenile fiction. | Contests—Juvenile fiction. |
Video games—Juvenile fiction. | CYAC: Superheroes—Fiction. |
Supervillains—Fiction. | Animals—Fiction. | Contests—Fiction. | Video
games—Fiction.
Classification: LCC PZ7.1.F585 Sq 2020 | DDC [Fic—dc23 LC record available at https://lccn.loc.gov/2019007651

10 9 8 7 6 5 4 3 2 1   20 21 22 23 24

Printed in China   62
First edition, January 2020
Edited by Katie Carella and Alli Brydon
Book design by Maria Mercado

TABLE OF
CONTENTS

SUPER
ALL-STAR
GAMES

PRESS START

START
SELECT

It is a Tuesday in Animal Town. The animals are having a party to celebrate.

Suddenly, a star-shaped doorway appears in the sky! A star-shaped creature flies through it.

TO SUPER RABBIT BOY,

   YOU ARE INVITED TO THE SUPER
ALL-STAR GAMES TOURNAMENT! HEROES
AND VILLAINS FROM DIFFERENT WORLDS
WILL FACE MANY CHALLENGES.

   WHO WILL BE CROWNED THE ULTIMATE
ALL-STAR CHAMPION? MAYBE IT WILL
BE YOU!

   WILL YOU JOIN THE FUN? PLEASE
SAY YES.

CHEERS,
KING ALL-STAR

The starby has more invitations to give out.

The starby opens a new doorway.

Super Rabbit Boy and his friends arrive at the Super All-Star Games.

11

The starby shows them around.

We have gathered All-Stars from many different worlds.

12

A giant voice booms
down from above.

Welcome to the Super All-Star Games!

It's King All-Star!

A very special welcome to every All-Star.

Who will be crowned the Ultimate All-Star Champion? There is only one way to find out. Let the games begin!

Super Rabbit Boy wants to win!

Boing! Boing! Let's go!

3 ROUND ONE

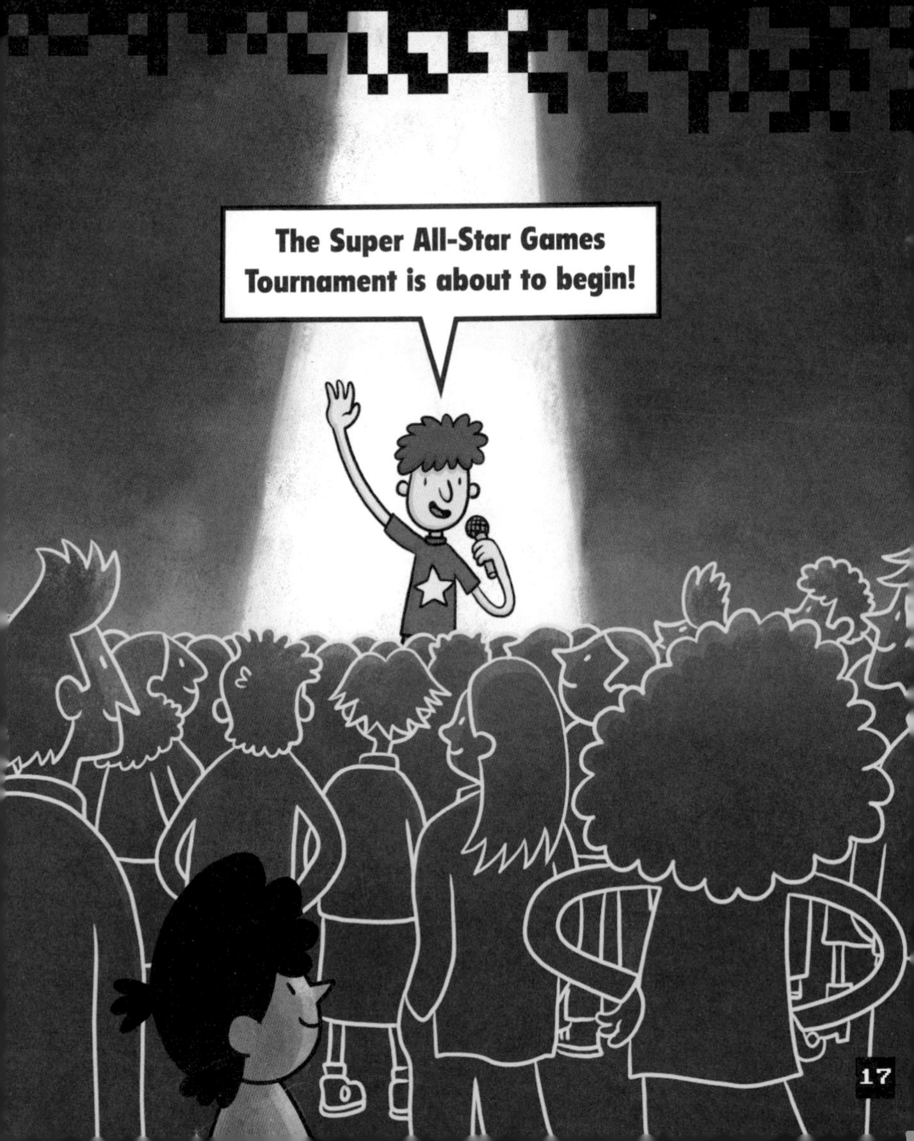

This is how the tournament works: There will be four rounds of games. You will all compete in the first round. Many games will be happening at the same time.

There will be ten players in each game. Only two players from each game will win. Those winners will move to the second round of games. Everyone else will leave the tournament.

After the second round — when only ten players are left — we will have the third round, or semifinal game. The two winners of the semifinal will play the final game. The winner of the final will be the Ultimate All-Star Champion!

Good luck!

Thanks!

The first game is . . .

Super Rabbit Boy is warped into his first game.

It's a race up Mega Mountain!

The first two players to reach the top will move to the next round!

Everyone speeds up the mountain. Who will get to the top first?

Super Rabbit Boy bounces. He is climbing quickly!

Some of the other racers struggle.

This race is too hard for Slimegirl. She can't jump!

Strong Boy is too slow for this challenge.

That is why I chose a character who can fly!

Super Rabbit Boy is surprised when Wingo flies past him.

See you at the top, bouncing bunny!

Oh bloop!

Just then, a big rock falls down the mountain. It crashes into Wingo!

Wing-NOOOO!

Mega Mole Girl peeks out of a hole.

Whoops! Sorry about that!

Hello, Mega Mole Girl!

Mega Mole Girl is digging a tunnel to the top of the mountain! She is super fast.

Sorry, Super Rabbit Boy. I can't chat now. I'm digging my way to victory!

Super Rabbit Boy is starting to understand that each All-Star has different powers.

I better move fast, or I'll lose this game and be knocked out of the tournament!

Super Rabbit Boy bounces higher and higher. The last part looks hard, but he can see the finish line!

Sky Guy and Angie Crow fly toward the top. They zoom past Super Rabbit Boy.

Super Rabbit Boy has an idea. He bounces off Angie Crow and Sky Guy toward the finish line.

Super Rabbit Boy is almost at the top of Mega Mountain!

Suddenly, Mega Mole Girl pops out of the mountaintop and wins the game!

Super Rabbit Boy makes it to the next round, too.

5 BUBBLE TROUBLE

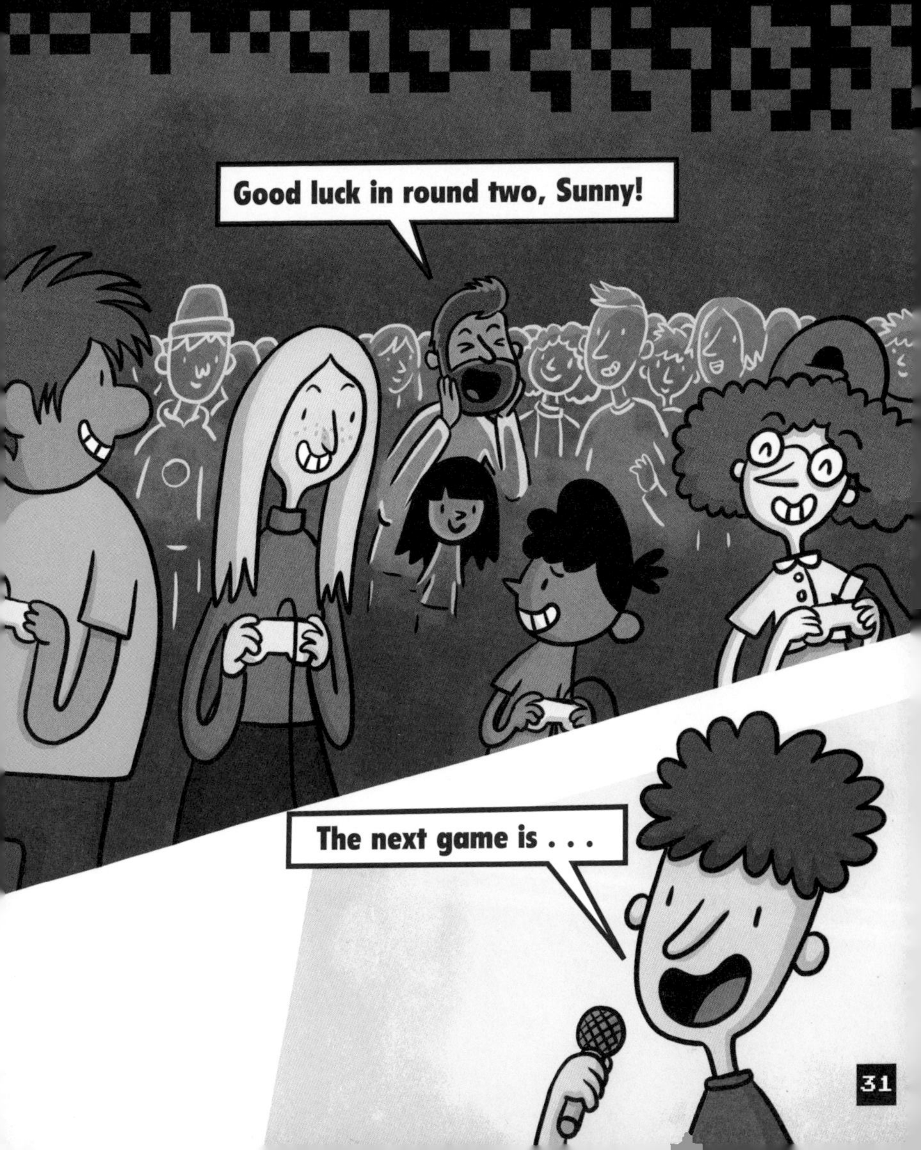

In a flash of light, Super Rabbit Boy is warped into his second game. He is floating inside a big bubble underwater.

The game starts with a whirl of action!
Mega Mole Girl gets thrown out of the
water first!

Super Rabbit Boy can't control his bubble
because he can't jump.

Pushington Bear swoops toward Super
Rabbit Boy.

Just before Pushington Bear can attack, he is grabbed by Crab Queen.

Crab Queen flings Pushington Bear out of the water <u>and</u> out of the game.

Crab Queen spots Super Rabbit Boy. He is her next target!

Before Crab Queen can grab Super Rabbit Boy, Gusty McCloud blows her out of the water!

Next, Gusty McCloud is bashed out of the water by Bashy Boy.

Bashy Boy, Super Rabbit Boy, and Worm Kid are the last three players in the game.

6 BASHING AND BOUNCING

Bashy Boy can't decide who to bash next: Super Rabbit Boy or Worm Kid.

I only need to bash one of you to win. Who will it be?

Super Rabbit Boy and Worm Kid are floating closer to each other. Suddenly, Super Rabbit Boy has an idea!

Hey, that's it! Worm Kid, keep drifting toward me!

I hope this is not a trick!

Bashy Boy sees Super Rabbit Boy and Worm Kid getting closer to each other.

I know! I'll bash both of you at once!

Bashy Boy zooms toward Super Rabbit Boy and Worm Kid.

Super Rabbit Boy uses his powerful jump to push away from Worm Kid's bubble.

Bashy Boy is going too fast to stop! He flies out of the water!

Bashy-baaaaaaaaaaaaaash!

Super Rabbit Boy and Worm Kid win the game!

Hooray!

That was a great idea, Super Rabbit Boy!

THE DANGER ZONE!

In a flash of light, Super Rabbit Boy is warped into the hardest game so far. It is full of obstacles, monsters, and traps.

46

47

Look! That man is using Billip!

I'm surprised he made it this far using such a weak character!

Those boys are using the Dude Bros. They have special dude moves.

3 . . .

2 . . .

1 . . .

Everyone jumps into action!
There are dangers everywhere.

King Jump
gets caught in
a spider's web!

Mister
Super Cool
falls through a
trapdoor!

King Viking is captured by a ghost gorilla!

Wah!

It flings him out of the tournament.

I'm too important to lose the game!

Super Rabbit Boy bounces past fireballs, jumping snakes, and spike pits.

The Dude Bros use their dude moves.

Billip appears in front of the Dude Bros.

Billip taps both Dude Bros with his glowing gloves.

Suddenly, the Ooze Monster attacks! The Dude Bros try to use their moves . . . but they can't.

Dude Flip? No?

Dude Slide? Huh?

Billip has stolen the Dude Bros' special dude moves! He flips and slides to safety. The Dude Bros are out of the game!

No way!

Not fair!

Wow! I did not know Billip can take powers from other characters and use them as his own!

That is what Billip does!

Super Rabbit Boy is getting tired. Luckily, he is far away from Billip.

Billip keeps stealing powers.

Without their powers, the other All-Stars
lose quickly.

The semifinal is over. Billip and Super Rabbit Boy made it through to the final!

Wow, that was fast! What happened to everyone?

Billip blip!

I'm surprised I made it!

Ha! No one is laughing at us now!

9 THE FINAL ROUND

The man using Billip is really good!

I told you Billip is a cool character!

Next up: the final round!

Go for it, Sunny!

In a flash of light, Super Rabbit Boy is warped into the final round of the Super All-Star Games!

Boing! Boing! Where am I now?

The final game is . . .

GRAB THE ALL-STAR CUP!

There can only be one Ultimate All-Star Champion!

Super Rabbit Boy and Billip race to find the All-Star Cup! Billip has lost the powers he stole in the last round.

Super Rabbit Boy leaps to a high platform.

He sees Billip down below.

Boing! Boing! Where is the All-Star Cup? I hope I can find it first!

He spots the cup. It is really high up!

There it is! I think I can reach it with my super jump.

Before Super Rabbit Boy can bounce, Billip appears. He taps Super Rabbit Boy with his glowing glove.

Super Rabbit Boy tries to jump, but he just falls down. He has lost his jumping power!

10 NORMAL RABBIT BOY

Sorry, kid. You did well to get this far. Now I am going to win!

I won't give up. The game isn't over yet!

Billip may have taken Super Rabbit Boy's power, but Billip doesn't know where the All-Star Cup is.

I can still win if I stay hidden.

Super Rabbit Boy can't jump anymore, so he climbs instead.

Even without my jumping power, I am still an All-Star.

Billip bounces around looking for the cup. He does not see it anywhere.

But Super Rabbit Boy keeps climbing. He is getting closer to the All-Star Cup!

Billip looks up and spots Super Rabbit Boy nearing the All-Star Cup. He uses his new jumping power.

Super Rabbit Boy climbs as fast as he can. But he is just a normal Rabbit Boy.

Billip has almost caught up to him.

Super Rabbit Boy has an idea. He lets go and falls into the air!

Super Rabbit Boy lands on top of Billip!
Together, Super Rabbit Boy and Billip zoom
toward the All-Star Cup.

They both
reach out and . . .

Super Rabbit Boy grabs the All-Star Cup first! He has won!

I did it!

THOMAS FLINTHAM

has always loved to draw and tell stories, and now that is his job! He grew up in Lincoln, England, and studied illustration in Camberwell, London. He lives by the sea with his wife, Bethany, in Cornwall.

Thomas is the creator of THOMAS FLINTHAM'S BOOK OF MAZES AND PUZZLES and many other books for kids. PRESS START! is his first early chapter book series.

These All-Stars are somewhere in the story. Can you find them all?

Spingy

Eye Guy

Astro Pete

Little Knight

Flame Kid

PRESS START!

How much do you know about
SUPER RABBIT ALL-STARS !?

All-stars from many different worlds are asked to join the Super All-Star Games Tournament. Who is invited from Animal Town?

Super Rabbit Boy is worried about the BUBBLE BOP game. Why does he think this game will be hard for him?

Who wins Mega Mountain Climb? How does this character win? Reread Chapter 4.

Who is the only character not cheering for Super Rabbit Boy at the end?

Super Rabbit Boy, Mega Mole Girl, Worm Kid, and Billip do well in the tournament. If you were Sunny, which character would you choose? Which game would you play? Write and draw your own action story.

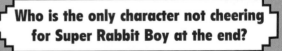